WALT DISNEY PRODUCTIONS
presents

# Goofy and the Pirate Treasure

Random House  New York

**GROLIER BOOK CLUB EDITION**

First American Edition. Copyright © 1980 by Walt Disney Productions
All rights reserved under International and Pan-American Copyright Conventions.
Published in the United States by Random House, Inc., New York,
and simultaneously in Canada by Random House of Canada Limited, Toronto.
Originally published in Denmark as FEDTMULE OG SØRØVERSKATTEN by
Gutenberghus Bladene, Copenhagen.
ISBN: 0-394-84538-2 (trade); 0-394-94538-7 (lib. bdg.)
Manufactured in the United States of America
D E F G H I J K      1 2 3 4

One day Mickey visited his friend Goofy
at Goofy's house by the sea.
Goofy told Mickey he had to sell his house.

"Oh no!" said Mickey. "Why?"
"I do not have enough money to fix up this old place," said Goofy.

"It is sad," said Goofy. "My family has lived here since the days of my great-grandfather, Goofy the Great. He was a famous pirate."

"A pirate!" said Mickey. "Did he ever hide any treasure?"

"Nobody knows," said Goofy.

"I have Goofy the Great's sea chest,"
said Goofy. "But it is full of old clothes.
I will show it to you."

The old chest was in the attic.
It was covered with cobwebs.
"I have never looked through all this
junk before," said Goofy.

"Wow!" said Mickey. "Look at this spyglass!"
"And here is a sword,"
said Goofy. "And
a pirate hat!"

They climbed to the top of Goofy's house.
Mickey brought the spyglass with him.
He looked up and down the seashore.

"I bet your great-grandfather hid treasure
out there somewhere," said Mickey.

"If we could find the treasure," said Goofy,
"then I would not have to sell my house."

FOR
SALE

Goofy and Mickey went back to the attic.
"If I were a pirate," said Goofy, "I would
know how to find the treasure."
He sliced the air with his pirate sword.

Then Mickey found an old, rolled-up paper.
"It is a treasure map!"
cried Mickey.

"So there really
is a hidden pirate
treasure!" said Goofy.

Find treasure near trees, near rocks, near water. My message goes in circles—and so shall you! Signed: Captain Goofy

Beach

Trees

Rocks

Mountains

Beach

Ocean

River

River

Mountains

River

River

Lake

River

Mountains

Rocks

Trees

Rocks

Beach

Ocean

"This map
will not
be easy
to follow,"
said Mickey.
"But we have
to try to find
the treasure."

They loaded Goofy's jeep with lots of supplies.
They packed cots, a cooking stove, food,
and pots and pans.

Goofy brought picks and shovels to dig
for the treasure.

He even wanted to bring
an alarm clock.

Finally Goofy brought out a grandfather clock. "Stop, Goofy!" said Mickey. "We have too many things already."

"But we might need this tent," said Goofy.

"And a rubber raft could come in handy,"
he added.

Finally they were ready to go.
They hoisted their pirate flag, the Jolly
Roger, and started off.

Mickey and
Goofy drove
along the seashore
until they came
to a river.
"There are rocks and trees
on the other side of the river,"
said Goofy. "I bet the treasure
is buried over there."

So they unloaded all their camping supplies
at the edge of the river.

Mickey and Goofy put their supplies
into the rubber raft.
There was almost no room left
for the two of them.

Mickey and Goofy
paddled hard.
Finally they reached the
other side of the river.

Mickey and Goofy walked until they
came to the ocean again.

Then they took another look at the map.

"My pirate blood tells me that the
treasure is up on top of that cliff,"
said Goofy. "There are trees up there—
and a big rock."

First they got some of their supplies.
Then they climbed up the steep cliff
at the edge of the ocean.

When they got to the top of the cliff,
Goofy spotted a cave on the other side.

Mickey tied a rope around Goofy and
lowered him down to the cave.

"This has to be where the treasure is
hidden," said Goofy. "I am going inside."

"I am coming, too!" said Mickey.

The cave was dark and scary.
Goofy was glad he had his lantern.

The cave turned into
a narrow tunnel. And the
tunnel went straight down!

Mickey lowered himself to the bottom.
He saw lots of frogs.
But he did not see any treasure.

Goofy came down to the bottom, too.

"I do not like this," said Goofy. "I want to go back."

"Not now," said Mickey. "I hear the sound of water ahead of us."

At the end of the dark tunnel they could see the ocean.

They came out of the cave and made
a fire on the beach.

It was dark and they were tired and hungry.

"We can sleep on the beach tonight,"
said Mickey. "Tomorrow morning we will
find our way home."

Early the next morning, Goofy and Mickey
walked back to the rubber raft.

They had given up their treasure hunt.

They paddled back across the river.

"That map was stupid," said Goofy angrily.
"There are rocks and trees around my house,
too. But there is no treasure there."

They drove back to Goofy's house.
"I still have no money," said Goofy.
"So now I have to move out of
my house."

Mickey helped
Goofy carry the
rest of Goofy's
furniture out of
the house.

"Whew!"
said Mickey,
when the jeep was
loaded. "I hope we
have everything."

"All but the pirate chest,"
said Goofy. "That is
empty now, so it will
not be heavy."

Goofy and Mickey went up to the attic
to get the pirate chest.

But the chest was too heavy to move.

"Gosh," said Mickey. "This thing must be
made of lead!"

Goofy was ready to try again.

But Mickey saw a shiny place on the side
of the chest.

"Wait!" Mickey cried. "I think this chest
is made of gold! Let us scrape off the paint."

Soon the chest was gleaming.
"Mickey, it is true!" cried Goofy.
"The chest is made of gold. I am rich!"
Mickey smiled at his friend.
"Goofy the Great's map was right
after all," said Mickey.

The two friends soon moved all of Goofy's things
back into the old house.

Then they got a big crane to come and lift
the heavy chest out of the attic.

An armored truck took the gold chest to the bank.

"Goofy, now you will not have to
sell your house," said Mickey.

Goofy used part of his money
to fix up his old house.

He built a new porch.

He painted everything.

And he put up a new flagpole so that he
could fly the Jolly Roger—the pirate flag
of Goofy the Great.